For Lily and Isla—A.L.

OXFORD
UNIVERSITY PRESS

Great Clarendon Street, Oxford OX2 6DP

Oxford University Press is a department of the University of Oxford.
It furthers the University's objective of excellence in research, scholarship,
and education by publishing worldwide. Oxford is a registered trade mark
of Oxford University Press in the UK and in certain other countries

Text and Illustrations copyright © Alex Latimer 2023

The moral rights of the author have been asserted

Database right Oxford University Press (maker)

First published in 2023

British Library Cataloguing in Publication Data

Data available

ISBN: 978-0-19-278386-8

1 3 5 7 9 10 8 6 4 2

Printed in China

Paper used in the production of this book is a natural,
recyclable product made from wood grown in sustainable forests.
The manufacturing process conforms to the environmental
regulations of the country of origin.

Ray

Alex Latimer

OXFORD
UNIVERSITY PRESS

It had been such a lovely day for a walk . . .

. . . that Mouse didn't realise
how late it was getting.

And in no time,
the sun had set.

Mouse was terrified.

'How will I ever get home
safely in the dark?' he sobbed.

But then there came a glow from inside a flower . . .

. . . which grew
brighter, and
brighter,
and brighter,
until . . .

POP!

. . . out popped a firefly. 'Follow me,' she said.
'I'm Ray and I'll light your way!'

'Oh, thank you!' said Mouse.
'But just so you know, I'm not *actually*
scared of the dark. It's just that tonight
the moon isn't as bright as usual,
so it's tricky to see.'

My house is past the woodpile . . .

. . . around the cactuses . . .

...up by the pond...

...and just beyond the rocks.

home

'Follow me,' said the firefly.
'I'm Ray and I'll light your way!'

So Mouse followed until . . .

'A SNAKE. I'M TOAST!'

Then Ray flew closer and said . . .

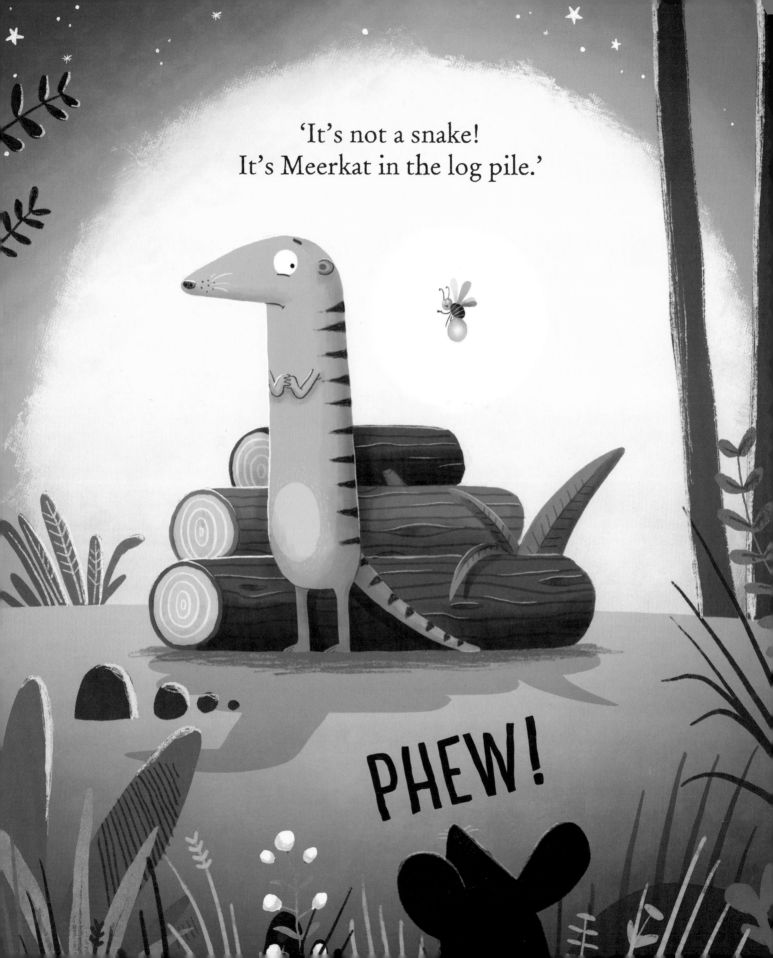

'It's not a snake!
It's Meerkat in the log pile.'

PHEW!

But Meerkat didn't want to stay in the log pile.

'Can I join you?
I'm *definitely NOT* afraid of the dark,
but I am . . . um . . . allergic to starlight.'

'Of course,' said the firefly.
'I'm Ray and I'll light your way!'

So Mouse
and Meerkat
followed until . . .

'A BEAR!
WE'RE DONE FOR!'

Then Ray flew closer
and said . . .

'It's not a bear!
It's the hens roosting
in the cactuses.'

PHEW!

But the hens didn't want to stay in the cactuses.

'Can we join you? *Cluck!*
We're *TOTALLY* fine with darkness,
it's just that our . . . um . . .
favourite show is on TV, but Henrietta
here lost the . . . um . . . remote control.
We might as well watch at Mouse's!'

'Of course,' said the firefly.
'I'm Ray and I'll light your way!'

So Mouse,
Meerkat,
and the hens
followed until . . .

'A CROCODILE!
WE'LL BE DINNER FOR SURE!'

Then Ray flew closer
and said . . .

'It's not a croc!
It's five green frogs by a big log.'

PHEW!

But the frogs didn't want to stay by the pond.

'Can we join you? *Ribbit!*
We're *very* brave frogs and we *LOVE* the dark.
It's just that we enjoy a bit of tea before bed
and we don't have a kettle.'

'Of course,' said the firefly.
'I'm Ray and I'll light your way!'

So Mouse, Meerkat, the hens,
and the frogs followed until . . .

'A FOX!
IT'LL SNAP US UP!'

Then Ray flew closer
and said . . .

'It's not a fox!
It's three squirrels on the rocks.'

PHEW!

But the squirrels didn't want to stay on the rocks.

'Can we join you? The dark is *GREAT*.
But we were just on our way to Mouse's house
to borrow some . . . um . . . peanut butter.
So we may as well come with you.'

'Of course,' said the firefly.
'I'm Ray and I'll light your way!'

So Mouse,
Meerkat,
the hens,
the frogs,
and the squirrels followed . . .

. . . until . . .

'A LION!'

said Mouse.

'Wait. No. Hold on . . .

. . . that's not a lion at all!
That's my home.

The legs are just tree trunks.
The mane is just leaves.
The tail is just a reed.
We're safe now!

Go on, Ray, show them.'

So Ray flew closer . . .

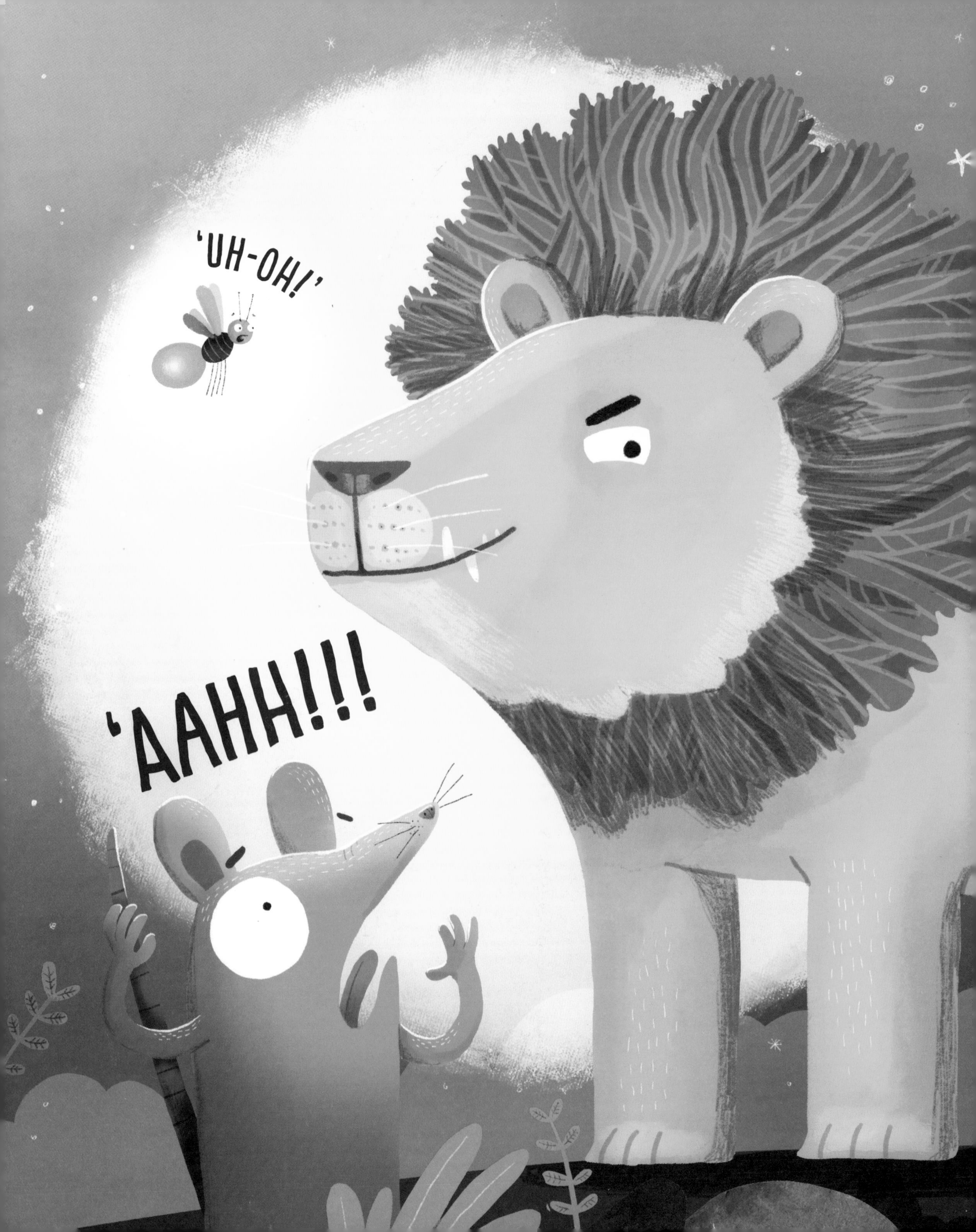
'UH-OH!'
'AAHH!!!

IT *IS* A LION!'

Mouse opened his eyes. It was very dark.

'Ray?' Mouse called.
'I *am* afraid of the dark.'

'Me too.'

'And me.'

'Same here.'

'We all are.'

We need you, Ray.
We need you
to light the way.'

Then there came a glow that grew . . .

. . . brighter

and brighter

and brighter!

'Oh dear!' said Mouse.

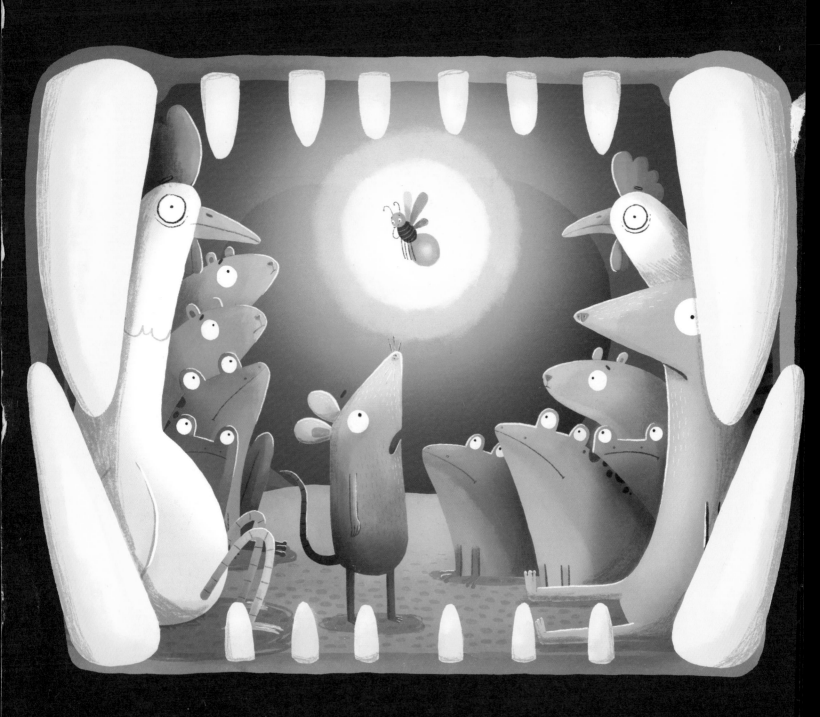

'How do we get out of here?'

'Follow me,' said the firefly.
'I'm Ray and I'll light your way!'